GROSSET & DUNLAP
Published by the Penguin Group
Penguin Group (USA) Inc., 375 Hudson Street, New York, New York 10014, USA
Penguin Group (Canada), 90 Eglinton Avenue East, Suite 700,
Toronto, Ontario M4P 2Y3, Canada
(a division of Pearson Penguin Canada Inc.)
Penguin Books Ltd., 80 Strand, London WC2R 0RL, England
Penguin Group Ireland, 25 St. Stephen's Green, Dublin 2, Ireland
(a division of Penguin Books Ltd.)
Penguin Group (Australia), 250 Camberwell Road, Camberwell, Victoria 3124, Australia
(a division of Pearson Australia Group Pty. Ltd.)
Penguin Books India Pvt. Ltd., 11 Community Centre, Panchsheel Park,
New Delhi—110 017, India
Penguin Group (NZ), 67 Apollo Drive, Rosedale, North Shore 0632, New Zealand
(a division of Pearson New Zealand Ltd.)
Penguin Books (South Africa) (Pty.) Ltd., 24 Sturdee Avenue,
Rosebank, Johannesburg 2196, South Africa

Penguin Books Ltd., Registered Offices:
80 Strand, London WC2R 0RL, England

Illustrated by Andrew Grey. Text by Laura Dollin.

Library of Congress Cataloging-in-Publication Data is available.

ISBN 978-0-448-45334-7   10 9 8 7 6 5 4 3 2 1

Hooray for Friends!

Grosset & Dunlap
An Imprint of Penguin Group (USA) Inc.

Pooh Goes Visiting

One fine afternoon,
Pooh was walking through
the Hundred Acre Wood.
As he walked, he hummed a
little hum to himself.
He had thought it up that
very morning as he was
doing his stoutness exercises.

Tra-la-la, tra-la-la . . .

Pooh was hoping
to share his new
hum with someone,
when he came to a
sandy bank. In the
bank was a large hole.

"Rabbit lives inside that hole!" cried Pooh. "And that means someone to listen to my hum. And someone with food."

But when Pooh called out to Rabbit, Rabbit pretended that he wasn't at home. Rabbit even said that he was away visiting Pooh!

"That's me," said a very surprised Pooh.

"Oh, come in then," said Rabbit.

So Pooh **squashed** and **squeezed** his way through the hole, and was very pleased when Rabbit asked him if he would like something to eat.

Pooh couldn't decide between honey or condensed milk, so he said yes to both.

After all, it was nearly eleven o'clock in the morning, and Pooh always liked a little something at that time of the day.

At last, after checking that there was no food left, Pooh thanked Rabbit with a sticky voice, and said that he must leave.

He started to climb out of the hole.

He pulled and **pushed**, until his nose, ears, and front paws were in the open . . .

and then . . .

nothing . . .

"Oh, help and bother!" said Pooh. "I can't move."

By now, Rabbit had gone
out of his back door, and round
to the front to see Pooh.
"Give me your paw,"
he said, and Rabbit pulled,
and pulled,
and pulled . . .

"Ouch!" cried Pooh. He was stuck, and Rabbit knew why.

"I didn't want to say anything. But you've eaten too much," he said. "I shall see if Christopher Robin can help."

So, Rabbit brought Christopher Robin, who quickly saw that there was only one thing to do.

"We'll have to wait for you to get thin again, so we can pull you out," he said.

Pooh was very anxious. He would have to stay there for a week without any food.

He began to sigh and then a tear rolled down his cheek.

"Would you read a sustaining story to help and comfort me?" he said.

"Of course, you Silly old Bear," said Christopher Robin.

And every day, he read to Pooh, while Pooh felt himself getting slimmer and slimmer.

Until, at the end of the week, Christopher
Robin took hold of Pooh's front paws, and Rabbit
and all his friends and relations took hold of
Christopher Robin, and they pulled together.

With a sudden "Pop!" they all fell
backward and out came Pooh—free at last.

Pooh nodded to his friends and then continued his walk through the Forest, humming proudly to himself.

Tra-la-la.

Eeyore Has a Birthday

"Good morning, Eeyore!" said Pooh cheerfully.

"Good morning, Pooh Bear," replied Eeyore gloomily.

"If it is a good morning," he added.

"Oh dear, what's the matter?" said Pooh.

Eeyore explained that there was nothing,

absolutely nothing, not even a tiny thing
the matter, and that he really wasn't complaining,
for it couldn't matter less, and that he really shouldn't
be sad on his birthday.

"Your *birthday*?" said Pooh in surprise.

Eeyore said that of course it was his birthday and
couldn't Pooh see all the presents lying around and the
birthday cake with candles and pink icing?

Pooh was rather puzzled, for he couldn't see any
presents at all. Or, for that matter, any cake with
candles and pink icing.

"I can't see any of those things," he said.

And Eeyore grunted miserably
and agreed he couldn't see
them, either.

Pooh scratched his head and
wished Eeyore many happy
returns of the day, anyway.

Then, leaving Eeyore to mutter about nobody taking any notice of his birthday, Pooh hurried home as quickly as he could. He felt very sad about Eeyore and wanted to find him a present.

Outside Pooh's house, Piglet was jumping UP and down, trying to reach the knocker.

"Hello, Pooh!" said Piglet. "I was just coming to see you . . ."

"I've just seen Eeyore," interrupted Pooh. "And he's in a **Very Sad Condition** because it's his birthday and nobody has taken any notice. He's very Gloomy indeed. We must take him a present."

The two friends
went inside Pooh's
house and Pooh
went straight to his
honey cupboard to
see what he could
find. He had lots of
honey pots, but only
one with any honey
left inside!

"I'm going to give
this to Eeyore," he said proudly.

Piglet thought for a moment and then he
remembered that he had one balloon left
from his party. He would go and get it to
cheer up Eeyore.

And so Pooh set off with his jar of honey and Piglet trotted home to fetch the balloon.

It was a warm day, and Pooh began to get a funny feeling creeping over him, from the tip of his nose right down to the end of his toes.

He knew that feeling. It was a feeling that told him that it was time for a little something.

And, with that,
he sat down and
took the lid off his
jar of honey.

He began to eat,
and eat . . .
and eat.

And as he licked the last drop of honey, he
wondered where it was he had been going.

"Ah, yes, Eeyore!" he said. And then, "Bother!"
when he realized he'd eaten Eeyore's birthday
present. *What could Pooh give him instead?* He
thought for a while and then decided that the pot
was a very nice pot even without the honey inside,
and surely Eeyore might find it Useful.

Pooh continued on his way, and as he was passing Owl's house in the Wood, he called in to see him.

Showing Owl his Useful Pot for Eeyore, Owl said that he should write "A Happy Birthday" on it. Pooh thought that was a very good idea and asked Owl to help him.

Which he did, nodding wisely as he wrote:

HIPY PAPY BTHUTHDTH THUTHDA BTHUTHDY.

("A Very Happy Birthday with love from Pooh.")

Meanwhile, Piglet had
fetched his balloon and was
holding on to it very tightly
so that it wouldn't blow away.

He ran as fast as he could,
so that he might get to Eeyore before Pooh, and
thinking just how pleased Eeyore was going to be,
he forgot to look where he was going.

His foot landed in a rabbit hole and he fell flat
on his face.

BANG!!!!

For a moment, Piglet wondered what could have happened.

Had the Forest fallen down? Or had he blown up?

Perhaps he was far away on the moon . . . then he looked down and realized that it was *he* who had fallen down and that his poor balloon had popped and was now nothing more than a small piece of rag.

"Oh dear!" said Piglet. "Oh dear, oh dear, oh dearie dearie dear."

Now his present for Eeyore wasn't such a good one. Never mind, perhaps Eeyore didn't like balloons so very much, anyway? He would still take it to him, so he trotted on sadly to the stream where Eeyore was.

Eeyore was just gazing at his reflection in the water, concluding that it was a very sorry sight, when he heard Piglet's voice behind him.

"Good morning, Eeyore!" said Piglet. "And many happy returns of the day!"

Eeyore turned around gloomily and stared at Piglet.

"I've brought you a present!" continued Piglet excitedly. "It's a balloon!"

Eeyore could feel his gloom slipping away. Now that he was getting a balloon, it really did feel like a birthday. "But, Eeyore," continued Piglet. "I'm so sorry, so very, very sorry, I'm afraid when I was bringing it to you, I fell over and I burst the balloon," said Piglet.

There was a long silence.

"*My* balloon?" said Eeyore at last, and Piglet nodded.
He held out the little piece of damp rag. Eeyore looked
at it and Piglet felt really rather miserable. But Eeyore
didn't seem too upset and asked Piglet what color it
had been when it *was* a balloon. When Piglet told him
that it had been red, Eeyore said, "Thank you, Piglet.
My *favorite* color."

Just then, Winnie-the-Pooh arrived.

"Happy birthday, Eeyore!" Pooh called. "I've brought you a present, too." He gave Eeyore the Useful Pot and Eeyore became quite excited.

"Look, little Piglet!" Eeyore exclaimed. "I do believe that the balloon you gave me will fit very nicely into this rather Useful pot!"

Piglet looked on hopefully as Eeyore put the balloon in the pot.

"There you are!" said Eeyore.

And Pooh and Piglet were very happy indeed that Eeyore was so pleased with his presents.

In fact, when it came to say good-bye and happy birthday once again, Eeyore hardly noticed that his friends were going, for he was *far* too busy taking the balloon out and putting it back in again, happy as can be.

What a perfect present!